My Fine Feathers

STORYBOOK SERIES

Written by   J.L.W

My Fine Feathers
Copyright © 2020 by J. L. W

Tellwell Talent

www.tellwell.ca

ISBN

978-0-2288-2536-4 (Hardcover)

978-0-2288-2535-7 (Paperback)

This book is dedicated to everyone.

The Scarlet Macaws bright
primary colors scream at us to be

unapologetically bold and beautiful
just as we are!!!

Let your light shine, it's divine!

Lulu loves school. She enjoys her walk to school. She really likes Ms. Lane, her teacher and learning new things. Most of all, Lulu loves being with so many of her friends each day at school.

Today at school is show and tell. It is a special show and tell because her classmate KJ is bringing in his pet parrot to visit Lulu's class.

"Luluuuuuu!" Lulu hears her dad calling up from downstairs.

"The school bells going to ring, ding a ling!!!" Dad sings. Lulu's dad loves to turn sentences into songs.

After breakfast, Lulu and her dad head out for Lulu's school. Aunt B, Lulu's loving pup, comes too.

Today is a warm day, and there are lots of puddles because it rained last night. Lulu loves puddles. "No puddle jumping before school Lulu", Dad reminds her. "You will get wet and muddy."

Dad and Aunt B wave goodbye at the fence as Lulu runs to meet up with her friend Maddy. Maddy greets Lulu excitedly, but Lulu is suddenly distracted. She spots something out of the corner of her eye.

There, sitting in a puddle, is a big green frog. Lulu cannot resist. She tiptoes over, and pounces with a splash, aiming for the slippery frog. The frog jumps away with a *ribbet*, unaffected.

Uh oh, Lulu's once clean school clothes are now dripping with muddy water.

"Eww Lulu", Maddy laughs as the school bell rings.

Lulu is not concerned. She shakes off whatever water she can as she skips to the doors of the school.

Inside the school's hallway, some of Lulu's classmates look at her with shocked wide eyes. Lulu does not mind. She heads inside to her classroom.

Ms. Lane pipes up, then sings her usual "Good morning friends. It's a new day. Another gift for joy and play."

Maddy and her classmates take their seats.

"We have a special visitor today", says Ms. Lane. She introduces KJ's dad.

KJ's dad is carrying something big covered with a blanket. Lulu and her classmates are excited to see what is underneath.

"I want to show you a picture of the beautiful bird I fell in love with and decided to bring home to be a part of my family." KJ's dad holds up a large picture of a bald, sick looking bird.

"That looks like Lulu after she jumped in the puddle", Kyle remarks and some of the class giggle.

Lulu scrunches her nose and crosses her arms in front of her, "Hmph."

From under the blanket, a distinct voice says, "I'm special, I'm special".

Who is that talking? The class wonders.

Lulu and her classmates are mesmerized. KJ's dad smiles. "This is part of the reason I was smitten with this bald bird," he says. "I knew she was special inside and out. I was willing to see how special Scarlet is on the inside. Her unique beauty shone through, just as each of us shines from within".

"I'd like you to meet Scarlet" KJ's dad says as he takes the blanket off of the cage.

Lulu and her classmates are amazed. "Wow", Lulu and Maddy say together, then giggle.

Scarlet is beautiful. Her feathers are bright and colourful.

"Each of us has unique qualities," says Ms. Lane. "We are all special in our own way. Just like Scarlet has lots of fine colorful feathers now, we each have our own special colorful feathers that make us who we are."

"I'm special, I'm special" Scarlet chimes in. Lulu and her classmates giggle.

"Today," says Ms. Lane, "we are going to decorate the fine feathers of our classmates. Let's tell each other what special qualities we see in one another. What colorful light shines from within each of us?"

Kyle gives Lulu a bright red feather that says "adventurous" on it. This makes Lulu happy.

At the end of the school day, Lulu runs to Dad and Aunt B who are waiting by the fence to the school yard. She waves her fan of colorful feathers at them, each one labeled by a classmate describing Lulu's unique inner beauty.

Lulu waves her fan as she skips home next to Dad and Aunt B. "I'm special", she says.

"Let your light shine," adds Dad. "It's divine. Embrace your colors. You're a rainbow scholar".

Lightning Source UK Ltd.
Milton Keynes UK
UKHW050621230720
367029UK00007B/98